Biggie the Bear

CARES

How Biggie the Bear Learned to:

Cooperate

Appreciate

Respect others

Encourage efforts

Speak up

Biggie the Bear CARES:
Stories about Success Skills

<u>Introduction for Parents,</u>

<u>Grandparents, Teachers &</u>

<u>Counselors</u>

(11/11/19)

Biggie the Bear stories teach important social and emotional lessons to 5 to 9 year-old children. Stories describe how Biggie faced his fears and tamed his temper. Stories also tell how Biggie learned to: take turns; be appreciative; try hard; and, speak up to warn before he blew up. By learning to Cooperate, Appreciate, Respect others, Encourage efforts and Speak up calmly, Biggie became a Bear that CARES.

Parents can read stories aloud and discuss them with their children. However, it is especially effective to "tell" the stories and act them out. To try this approach, first pre-read and visualize a story, so you can "tell" it by narrating the images in your memory. As you tell the story, try to dramatize it with your voice tone and facial expressions.

Grandparents who live far away can record and send stories to their grandchildren. Discussions about story lessons could then occur during phone conversations or grandparent visits.

Teachers and counselors can present stories to groups of students and discuss lessons that stories teach.

CARES *Success Skills for Kids* (also by Dr. Bob Peddicord) gives detailed descriptions of CARES Success skills, along with explanations of their importance to getting along with others and developing social-emotional maturity. Also included are practice programs and games to promote learning of each of the CARES skills, along with guidelines for identify skills a particular child needs to be more successful.

Important Message to Give to Children

Help children understand that the story of Biggie the Bear is imaginary. Children should not approach wild animals, such as bears. They are not safe to touch and do not make good pets. If you or a child find a baby animal in the woods, it is best to "leave it there" and leave it alone! The mother may be close by, or getting food for her young.

If the animal looks hurt or sick, a child should stay away from it and tell a grown-up. The grown-up can then contact the warden service for help.

The 24-hour phone number for
the warden service in Maine is:
1-800-452-4664

4

Copyright

ISBN-13:978-1533415868

ISBN-10:1533415862

Contents

The True Story of Biggie the Teddy Bear

When Dr. Bob and his family were on a ski vacation at Sugarloaf Mountain in Maine, Dr. Bob's two year-old son Scott came into the parents' room because he

7

was sleeping in another room and was
lonely. Dr. Bob picked up Scott's teddy bear
and started telling him stories about an
imaginary black bear named Biggie the
Bear. Over the coming years, Dr. Bob told
many stories about how Scott and Biggie
the Bear helped each other and became
very good friends.

Later, Dr. Bob made up stories for
children about how Biggie the Bear
learned to face his fears and tame his
temper. Biggie also learned how to take
turns, try hard, and speak up before he
blew up. Those stories are in this book.

The Imaginary Story of Biggie the Bear

One summer day, two kids were sitting on a big rock with their dad and looking out over a lake. A cute little bear cub came down a path. The kids wanted to pet the little bear, but their dad said "No," because it's not safe to pet a wild animal and a mother bear might be nearby. She would be very angry if she thought someone was bothering her cub. Therefore, the kids and their dad hurried back to their cottage by the big lake. When the boy named Scott looked over his shoulder, he saw the little bear following them. Back at the cottage, the parents reminded the kids not to try to pet a wild animal because it isn't safe, especially if there might be an angry mama bear around.

However, when Scott looked out the window later, he saw the little bear sitting on a rock. He said, "That baby bear looks so hungry. Can we give it some food?" The parents said, "Let us check around first and put out some food to make sure it's safe."

After the grown-ups put out some food
and saw that it was safe, Scott and his
sister Sara put out food every day for the
baby bear, that they called "Little Bear."

They gave it blueberries they had picked and a bowl of milk.

When the family was ready to go back to their home in the city, Scott said, "Little Bear looks lonely. Can we bring him home with us and take care of him?"

The parents thought about it and the mom said, "Bears belong in the woods, but we will find out how to safely take care of him until he is big enough to go back and live in the woods."

The kids were happy because Little Bear was so friendly. When they got home, the kids took turns each night sleeping with Little Bear. One night, Scott cuddled with him and hugged him. The next night, Sara laid her head on Little Bear's furry back and used it as a soft and warm pillow.

The kids had many fun adventures with Little Bear and took good care of him. He became their "little buddy bear."

How Little Bear Learned to Stay Safe

One time, when Little Bear saw a furry black animal in the backyard and wanted to play with it, the kids yelled "No, No, Little Bear!"

Unfortunately, Little Bear didn't listen and he got sprayed by the skunk. He became "Stinky Bear" and had to have many baths. After that, he learned to listen to the kids and stop when they told him to.

That winter, they were at the family's cottage, along with friends of the kids and their dog. They were playing near the lake that had just frozen over when Little Bear started to follow the dog onto the thin ice. Scott and Sara shouted, "No, Little Bear!" This time the Little Bear listened and stopped, just as the ice cracked under the dog, sending it scurrying back to shore. When the parents saw the kids helping Little Bear stop, they complimented them for keeping him safe. Little Bear would have been very cold if he had fallen through the thin ice.

How Little Bear Became Biggie the Bear

After Little Bear lived with the kids for a couple of years, he rescued Sara when she chased a ball into the street. He saw a car coming and quickly ran out to grab her sweatshirt in his teeth, as he pulled her out of the way.

Scott saw what happened and said, "That was such a brave thing to do and Little Bear is much bigger now. We should call him Biggie the Bear."

That is how **Biggie the Bear** got his name.

Soon afterwards, it became time for Biggie the Bear to go back and live in the woods. Scott and Sara's parents drove him to the woods behind the family's cottage at the lake, and the family said good-bye to Biggie.

He then searched until he found a bear cave where he could sleep at night, a stream where he could drink and catch fish, and wild blackberries that he could eat.

How Biggie Learned to
Face his Fear

When Biggie was still a little bear and lived with the family, he was afraid of the dark in the family's big old house. But, Scott and Sara taught him to face his fear. First, they showed Little Bear how to stop and take some slow deep breaths to calm down and relax. Then, they taught him how to use a flashlight to "chase the dark away." Sara took Little Bear's paw and Scott lead the way with a flashlight, which he pointed into dark places to "chase the dark away." Then, Little Bear held the flashlight in his mouth and "chased the dark away" by himself, as he went around the house to all the dark places all *upstairs* and down *stairs* and *into* the dark basement. By stopping to take some slow deep breaths and going slowly, Little Bear built up his courage and was able to face his fear of the dark. Afterwards, he felt proud of himself for facing that fear.

However, when the kids started back to school in the fall, Little Bear had to sleep alone in his own room, and he had trouble falling asleep. First, Scott and Sara put a nightlight in his room. Then, Sara remembered when she had trouble falling asleep alone and her mother stayed with her while she fell asleep, until Sara was ready to try it on her own. After that, Sara and Scott sat in Little Bear's room while he fell asleep. They stayed every night until he seemed ready to try it on his own. When he seemed ready, the kids showed Little Bear how to take some slow deep breaths and remember fun things from the day to help him relax. Then, they quietly left his room. After they left, Little Bear continued to take some slow deep breaths, as he remembered running through the woods with the kids, where he got stuck on a log until the kids helped him down.

The happy memory helped him fall asleep to a pleasant dream of being stuck on a log and the kids helping him get down.

After he became Biggie the Bear and went back to live in the woods, he was afraid the first night that he slept alone in his bear cave because the wind blew outside the cave and made the trees dance like mean dragons in the moonlight. Then, Biggie took some slow deep breathes and slowly remembered having fun with the kids. He drifted off to sleep and had a dream about playing with the kids in the woods.

Whenever Biggie wanted to face a fear, he would take some slow deep breaths and go slowly. When he overcame the fear, it made him feel proud of himself for being brave and trying hard.

Biggie says:

Face your Fear

Take slow deep breathes
to build up your courage,
and go slowly to
face your fear.

How Biggie Learned to
Tame his Temper!

When Biggie was still a little bear, he had
a terrible temper. One time at the cottage
by the lake, while he was eating some
berries and drinking some milk, a field
mouse came up to the bowl and started
drinking the milk. Little Bear was

furious! He swatted at the mouse, but missed it. Instead, he hit the bowl and broke it, spilling all the milk on the ground. He felt awful and was too embarrassed to ask for some more milk.

Later, when he and Scott were playing, Little Bear got angry because Scott was tickling him. He swatted at Scott and his sharp claws scratched Scott's arm. Whenever he saw the scratches on Scott's arm, Little Bear felt terrible. His temper had again made him do something he felt awful about, so he wanted to stop his temper!

Later, Little Bear and Scott were down at the park. A wild and frisky dog was pulling its master all over the place. That dog reminded Little Bear of his temper.

However, another bigger and more powerful dog was also much tamer. When he started to get too excited, his master would stop and take a break until that dog calmed down. Then, that dog would follow his master's lead.

Little Bear wanted to his to stop his
temper and tame it to become its "master"
so he could decide what he wanted to do,
rather than letting his temper decide.

Scott also knew that Little Bear needed to
learn to stop his temper, and he

remembered how his dad had used a **STOP** signal to help Scott learn to stop and take a break. So, Scott gave Little Bear a **STOP** signal whenever he saw him getting too angry.

When he saw the **STOP** signal, Little Bear stopped and took a break. Later, when Scott was not around, Little Bear *remembered* the **STOP** signal so he could stop himself when he got too angry.

Sometimes, he also gave himself a bear hug, as he recalled how his mother would hug him to hold him back when he was a baby bear and got too upset.

To help Little Bear also learn to calm down after he stopped, Scott showed him how to take some slow deep breaths. Then, they practiced taking slow deep breathes several times together. After that, whenever Little Bear got angry, he tried to remember to stop and take some slow deep breaths so he could calm down and think of a better plan.

One time, when Scott's friends were teasing Little Bear, he was able to stop his temper and calm down to ^think of a plan. He decided to growl at them before going off by himself to take a "private time." When Scott heard Little Bear growling, he told his friends to stop bothering Little Bear and leave him alone. Then Little Bear was able to have some peaceful "private time."

When he was able to stop his temper and calm down to think of a plan, Little Bear felt like a hero. In addition, the kids and their friends liked to play with him more because he was a gentler bear.

Later, Little Bear's tamed temper helped him become a gentle giant of a bear, named Biggie the Bear.

Be big like Biggie!

Tame your Temper!

To tame your temper:

STOP

1. Take a Biggie break.

2. Slowly take some deep Biggie breaths so you can calm down and pick a better plan.

How Biggie became
a Bear who
<u>CARES</u>

When Biggie lived with the kids, and later
when he moved back to the woods and
visited the kids, he had many experiences
that taught him important life lessons. He
learned how to take turns, be thankful,
respect peoples' stuff, try hard, stop to
think and speak up to warn. That's how
he became a Bear who <u>CARES</u>.

1. How Biggie Learned to Cooperate

How Biggie learned to listen to stay safe when he was a baby bear

When Biggie was a baby bear, his mother wanted him to stay in the den while she got some wild honey from a nearby tree.

However, he thought it would be fun to follow his mother. As he came up behind her, an angry bee stung him on his little nose. Then, another one stung him on his ear.

The painful experience and his mother's growl reminded the baby bear to listen to his mother. He was soon glad that he had learned the lesson.

One summer day the cub heard some loud --- Bang! Bang! noises outside his den. He was curious and wanted to see what the noises were, but his mother shook her head and motioned for him to stay in the den. This time the young bear listened to his mother. When the sound was further away, she motioned for him to look out of the den. As he looked, he could see some mean poachers off in the distance shooting at deer, which ran away from their scary "fire sticks."

The baby bear was glad that he had obeyed his mother. He could have been hurt if he had not listened to her.

How Little Bear learned
to take turns

When Little Bear lived with Scott and Sara, he sometimes wanted his way, right away, especially when he wanted to do something fun, like playing "Chase the Bear.'" He would start to run fast to get the kids to chase him and try to catch him. But, after playing the game for a while, the kids would often get tired and want to stop. However, Little Bear didn't want to stop and wait for another time. He would bug the kids to try to get them to play. He'd poke them with his nose and run circles around them to try to get them to chase him. Sometimes it worked, but the kids often got angry and told Little

Bear to leave them alone, especially when they had started doing something else. Then, Little Bear's feelings got hurt. One time, he swatted at the kids and just barely missed Sara's arm. Then, they all went inside to take a break.

While they were inside the mother asked why they weren't playing outside anymore. Sara explained that Little Bear wanted to play "chase the bear" all the time and got upset when the kids didn't want to play. The mother suggested they might have more fun if they took turns doing what each of them wanted to do.

When they went back outside, Scott and Sara showed Little Bear how to take turns. First they played "chase the bear" with him. Then, it was their turn and they chose to play "dress up the bear," as they put some of their hats and coats on him. Then, they played "chase the bear" again.

Little Bear learned to take turns and do what the kids wanted, to get to do what he wanted. Sometimes he would stand patiently for a long time and let Scott, Sara, and their friends play "Dress up the Bear."

Then, the kids and their friends would all play "chase the bear." They would even form teams and compete to see if they could catch Little Bear, but they almost

40

never could because he ran too fast and turned too quickly.

After he learned to take turns, the kids enjoyed playing with Little Bear more, and he was also more popular with their friends who would come to the cottage by the lake just to play with Little Bear.

When Little Bear and the kids took turns doing what each other wanted, they had great fun together!

How Little Bear and the kids took turns helping each other.

At the family's lake cottage, Scott taught Little Bear how to catch fish by throwing some bread on the water to bring fish up to the surface so Little Bear could catch them.

Little Bear also helped the kids learn to swim. He was a natural swimmer and helped the kids feel comfortable in the water by swimming slowly as they took turns stretching out on his back with their arms wrapped around neck. Later, the parents showed the kids how to add a frog kick, so they could swim along with their bear friend and eventually learn to swim on their own.

By taking turns at being the boss and helping each other, Little Bear and the kids had a "fair deal." They all got something they wanted and enjoyed being together.

How Biggie learned to pretend

One sunny afternoon, after Little Bear grew up and became Biggie the Bear, he came to visit Scott and Sara at the cottage by the lake. They were pretending to have a picnic. When Biggie saw the kids putting dishes on the table, it made him very hungry. He went over and sat down ready to eat. When the kids saw him sniffing the air, they realized that Biggie thought they were having a "real" picnic.

Sara said, "Oh, Biggie, we're just pretending!"

When Biggie looked puzzled, Scott said, "It's a make-believe-picnic."

Again, Biggie seemed confused, so Scott explained, "When we talk about your bear cave, you can imagine being there? That's like pretending."

Sara added, "You are pretending when you picture things in your mind and make-believe they're real."

Biggie looked surprised, as he understood what they meant. Then he had a pretend picnic with the kids. He even chomped his teeth as he ate make-believe corn and

Sell your books at sellbackyourBook.com!

Go to sellbackyourBook.com and get an instant price quote. We even pay the shipping - see what your old books are worth today!

Inspe

licked his lips after pretending to eat a
hot dog.

To celebrate Biggie learning to pretend,
the kids followed it with a **real** picnic.
Biggie was happy because he learned how
to pretend and he had a real picnic, too!

Be big like Biggie.

Cooperate by
Taking Turns
& Helping
Others.

Practice the "Fair Deal."

Take turns
"Being the Boss."

Help others, so they will help
you when you need it.

2. How Biggie Learned to Appreciate

When he was just a little bear, Biggie loved honey, but he couldn't always get it when he wanted it. One night, Little Bear heard a dog whining until its master let it in. The next time Little Bear wanted some honey he tried whining. Whining worked! He got the honey and was very happy. Then, the more he whined, the more he got, so he kept on whining until the kids gave in and gave him whatever he wanted. If they gave him something he didn't want, like cereal instead of honey, he whined loudly until he got the honey

But, Little Bear's whining annoyed the kids and they didn't want to play with him, which made him whine even more until they gave in and played with him.

When the parents saw this, they told the kids that Little Bear would keep on whining as long as they gave into his whining and gave him what he wanted. But, if they ignored his whining, he would have to find a better way to ask for what he wanted. Then, the mother added:

"I know it will be hard to ignore his whining, but try to remember you are doing it to help Little Bear learn a better way."

Sara then asked how they could help Little Bear learn. Her dad suggested,

"Wait until he asks nicely. Then, give him what he wants. That's why we often buy you a candy bar in a store when you ask nicely, even though we may save it for after dinner.

You can also teach Little Bear to be more appreciative by 'doubling his pleasure" and giving him more of what he wants when he is appreciative. That's why we often stay longer at the park to 'double your pleasure' when you thank us for taking you there."

Then, Sara asked how Little Bear could say 'thank you'?" Her dad explained that licking her hand might be Little Bear's way of saying "thank you."

When the kids started ignoring his whining, it was hard at first, especially because Little Bear whined longer and louder. His whining started to annoy the kids and they didn't want to be around him, which made them feel really bad and guilty. However, they kept on ignoring his whining and all that Little Bear got was frustrated.

When his whining wasn't working, Little Bear whined less, and the kids liked being around him more. Then, Scott and Sara showed Little Bear how to ask nicely for what he wanted. Scott looked at some popcorn, and then he looked at Sara to "ask" her nicely to give him some. He waited patiently to see whether she would give him some. If she did give him some popcorn, Scott smiled as he jumped up and down, which was a better way of thanking his sister than by licking her hand. Sara then gave him some more popcorn to "double his pleasure" because he was so appreciative.

Little Bear understood what the kids showed him. He then started asking nicely for something he wanted, and he showed appreciation if he got it. When he asked nicely, the kids quickly gave Little Bear what he asked for, along with a pat to thank him for asking so nicely. When Little Bear showed his appreciation, the kids "doubled his pleasure" by giving him even more of what he wanted.

Little Bear loved getting more of what he liked and getting positive attention too. They made getting what he wanted doubly sweet.

That is how Little Bear learned he got more of what he wanted in the long run when he asked nicely and appreciated, instead of whining and complaining.

To help Little Bear remember to thank them when they took him to the park, Sara would look at Little Bear and ask, "Why should we take you to the park if you don't show us you like it by thanking us?"

Little Bear usually understood, and thanked Sara by licking her hand and jumping up and down to show his appreciation. Then they all stayed at the park longer and had great fun playing together.

Sometimes, even when Little Bear asked nicely, the kids couldn't give him exactly what he ask for, but they tried to give him something they thought he would like. That is what happened when Little Bear looked at a picture of a bear in a book to ask nicely for a real "buddy" bear that he could play with. The kids talked to their parents and decided to give him a toy bear instead, which he loved and carried with him most of the time, especially when the kids played "Dress up the Bear."

To thank Little Bear for letting him, his sister and their friends play "Dress up the Bear," Scott would sometimes give Little Bear rides in his wagon, and Little Bear was able to take along his toy "buddy" bear for a ride.

The ride in the wagon helped Little Bear learn to show appreciation by doing nice things for the kids when they did nice things for him. Little Bear and the kids took turns doing nice things for each other, and they all got something they liked, which was also a "Fair Deal'.

Later when he was all grown up and lived in his bear cave, Biggie the Bear visited the family's cottage whenever he could. To show his appreciation for all the help they had given him, he often gave the kids rides on his back in the water. What fun the kids had riding on Biggie as he swam as fast as he could.

Best of all, Biggie enjoyed helping the kids have fun. He really cared about the kids, and it made him feel good when he could help them.

To show his appreciation to the parents for all they had done for him, Biggie also brought fish for them from the streams near his bear cave.

The parents grilled the fish, along with hot dogs for Biggie and the kids, which they all really enjoyed.

Be Big Like Biggie &
Appreciate

Say "Thank You"
and show appreciation.

3. How Biggie Learned to Respect Others

How Biggie learned to respect property and privacy

One time when Biggie visited the cottage he spotted what he thought was a bottle of honey on the picnic table. He quickly took a sip, but it tasted terrible! It wasn't honey. It was suntan oil! That is how Biggie learned to wait until Scott or Sara said it was okay to eat their food.

Another time in the camp, he saw a thing that had some peanut butter on it, but when he went to touch it, a mouse trap snapped on his claw. Although it didn't hurt him, it sure startled him and taught him to ask before he touched the family's stuff.

On another day, Biggie came around a corner of the cottage and ran up the stairs to the deck, which really scared some visitors who didn't know him, until the parents explained that he was a very friendly bear. However, Biggie was reminded that he needed to respect privacy and he remembered long ago when he lived with his mother and she taught him to wait and respect her privacy while she was feeding his brother. He would sometimes bug her and she would give him an angry growl. Then, when he waited, she would play with him and do what he wanted, which he really enjoyed.

Later when he visited the cottage, Biggie would approach more slowly so he didn't scare anyone, and he would wait when the kids were busy with their friends or when the parents were talking on the phone. The parents really appreciated it when Biggie respected their privacy on the phone and they would visit with him and cook hotdogs for him after they finished talking to their friends.

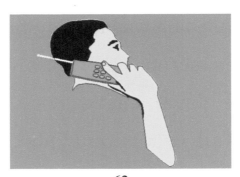

How Biggie learned to respect feelings

Biggie also respected other animals in the forest. He was very careful not to scare birds or other small creatures because he remembered how he felt when he was little and afraid. One time, a baby bird fell out of its nest high in a tree. Biggie let the bird ride on his shoulder as he climbed up the tree to take it back to its nest.

Biggie also tried to understand how others felt. Once, when he tried to save another baby bird, its mother angrily swooped down at him. Biggie didn't get upset because he understood that the

mother bird was just trying to protect her
young.

When he visited Scott and Sara, Biggie
learned to respect their feelings. When
Scott spoke to him, Biggie would look at
Scott's face to understand how he felt. If
Scott looked sad or mad, Biggie would
gently tilt his head to one side to "ask"
why his friend was upset.

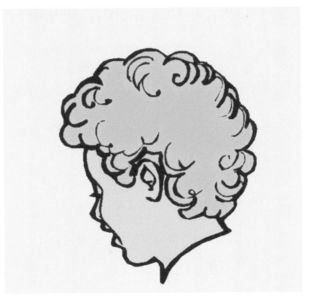

When Sara looked happy, as she did when Biggie brought her some flowers, it made Biggie feel good because he knew his kindness had made her feel good.

When he gave the kids rides on his back in the water and they laughed, it made him feel happy because he knew he had made them happy.

Biggie loved the kids and he knew they loved him when they gave him big hugs. He would respond with them very gentle bear hugs, which they loved, especially when it was getting cold outside and Biggie kept them warm.

Be Big Like Biggie.

Respect others

Respect others

Respect others'
Property, Privacy, and Feelings

1. Ask before you
touch other people's
things.

2. Wait when other
people are busy.

3. Look at people's
faces to understand
how they feel.

4. How Biggie Learned to Encourage Efforts

When Biggie was still a little bear and tried to learn new things, Scott gave him a pat on the back to *encourage* his efforts. Then, when Sara tried to ride a two-wheel bike, Little Bear jumped up and down to cheer her on and encourage her efforts.

How Biggie learned to be proud of himself when he tried hard.

Sara later encouraged Biggie to be proud of himself when he tried hard, even if he wasn't successful. One time when Sara was sick, Biggie went up into the woods to gather some flowers for her. He brought the flowers back and dropped them at her feet, but he felt awful when he saw that there were only the stems left.

He had knocked off all the flower buds as he brought them back through the bushes. However, Sara said, "Oh, Biggie, I'm so proud of you. You tried hard, and that's what's really important."

With her encouragement, Biggie felt better and was proud of his own efforts. But he wanted to figure out how to fix his mistake, so he took some deep breaths to calm down and think. He remembered that he had carried the flowers in his mouth as he brought them back through bushes. That is how the flower buds were probably knocked off from the stems! Biggie imagined a better plan. He decided to get some more flowers and carry them closer to his mouth, while pushing away the bushes with his paws.

When he tried again and brought flowers back to Sara, she said, "Oh, Biggie, I'm extra proud of you. You tried hard, and you learned from your mistake!"

Sara helped Biggie feel proud of himself when he tried hard and understand that mistakes are part of learning. Biggie also

found that he could learn from mistakes
when he thought about them and planned
how to fix them.

How Biggie learned to keep on trying

When he lived in his bear cave, he
dreamed of climbing the mountain above
the cave. However, he usually would go
around the long way to get to the top
where he could look out over the lake.

One day, Biggie decided to try to climb
the mountain. He noticed a long crack
going up the front of the mountain and
imagined shimmying up it. After he took
some deep breaths to calm down and be

brave, Biggie put his paws against one side of the crack and his back against the other side, as slowly began shimmy up the crack. Climbing this way was hard, but he kept on trying. However, when he was part way up, it started to rain and the crack began to get slippery. To be safe, Biggie decided to go back down, but he felt proud of himself for trying so hard.

The next day, he again tried to climb the mountain, but this time he went too fast and got tired. He decided to go back down to be safe. At first, he felt discouraged, but then he was proud of himself for trying hard.

By being proud of his efforts, Biggie was able to encourage himself and try again the next day. On the third day, Biggie went slowly and persisted until he finally reached the top, where he grabbed a tree root with his claws to pull himself up. As he stood on top of the mountain and looked out over the lake, he felt great and gave himself a big bear hug because he was finally successful.

By being proud of his own efforts, Biggie *encouraged* himself, which helped him try hard and keep on trying until he was successful.

How Biggie the Bear learned to work before he played

One day when Biggie came to the cottage by the lake, the kids were stacking wood for the winter. Biggie wanted to play, but Sara said, "Our parents taught us that we should work before we play, and then we can enjoy playing."

Biggie looked puzzled. Then, Scott said, "It's like when you had to work hard to find your bear cave in the woods before you could sleep well that first night."

Biggie understood and helped with the work by picking up sticks of wood with his teeth and giving them to Scott and Sara to stack. After they finished their work, Scott, Sara and Biggie played "Chase the Bear" and had great fun together. Then, they all swam in the lake to cool off.

That is how Biggie learned to work before he played so that he could really enjoy playing.

Be big like Biggie
Encourage Efforts.

Encourage efforts of
others and be proud of
your own efforts.

Encourage Efforts

1. Cheer others on.

2. Be proud of yourself when you try hard and keep on trying.

3. Work before you play, so you can really enjoy playing.

5. How Biggie Learned to Stop and Speak up

How Biggie learned to STOP

When Biggie the Bear was still a little bear, he felt frustrated when he wanted something and couldn't get it right away. This happened when Scott tried to teach him to fish. Scott threw a piece of bread on top of the water to attract a fish so that Little Bear could catch it. However, as soon as he saw the fish deep down in the water, Little Bear jumped in to catch it.

The fish quickly swam away and all Little
Bear got was wet!

Scott then taught Little Bear to stop and wait until the fish came up to the surface. He threw some more bread onto the water and put his arm in front of Little Bear to stop him until the fish came up to the top of the water to get the bread.

When the fish came up, Scott dropped his arm, and Little Bear jumped in and caught the fish. This helped him learn to stop and think when he wanted something really badly, but was getting frustrated.

How stopping to think helped Biggie

When Biggie the Bear lived in the woods, stopping to think helped him get some honey out of a log. He saw a honeycomb deep inside the log and stuck his tongue in to get it, but a bee stung him on his tender tongue.

Biggie got so frustrated and that he stuck his head in even further. Then, he got his head stuck in the log, and more bees stung his ear and his nose. When he pulled his head out of the log, the bees stung him all-over.

Biggie yanked at his nose and ears, and had a fit. He ran around through the bushes to let his frustration and anger out. Then, he jumped in a stream to cool down. However, even after his anger was out and he cooled down, he still wanted the honey. So, he took some deep breaths to blow out the rest of his frustration and think of a better plan.

He sat down on a rock to take a break. Then, he saw humming birds flying at a flower, first from one direction and then from another.

Biggie thought he might need to get to the
honey in a different way! Suddenly, he
imagined the log standing up on end. He
quickly ran over, picked up one end of the
log and banged on its side. As the
frightened bees flew away, the honeycomb

comb fell out and he was able to get to the honey and really enjoy it.

How Biggie learned to STOP and think when he was mad

Even after Biggie tamed his temper, his anger sometimes got the better of him. One day at the family's cottage by the lake, he was laying on the sunning rock by the water and enjoying the sun. The neighbor's dog came up, yapped at him and ran off. It happened over and over again. Each time, the dog came closer and closer to he pester Biggie. Finally, Biggie got so angry that he swatted at the dog, and it ran off yelping.

Scott saw what happened and told Biggie
to come into the family's cottage. After
Biggie came in, he looked out the window
and really got upset because the dog was
laying on Sunning Rock in the warm sun.

Scott's dad also saw the way Biggie
chased the neighbor's dog away, and he
was very concerned. After Biggie calmed

down, the dad talked to Scott. He explained that it was OK for Biggie to speak up by growling, but it was not OK for him to hurt people or their pets. If he did, the game warden might come and tell family Biggie couldn't visit anymore.

Scott agreed, and asked how he could help Biggie learn to speak up by growling, rather than hurting people or their pets. Scott's dad encouraged Scott to keep in mind that growling is Biggie's way of speaking up to say he does not like something. He explained further that Scott could help Biggie by listening to him and respecting his feelings whenever he growled.

Later, Scott decided to help Biggie practice speaking up. He knew that Biggie sometimes liked being tickled, but it bothered him at other times. Therefore, he tickled Biggie to see whether he liked it. If Biggie growled, Scott immediately respected his feelings and stopped. Then, he gave Biggie a pat on the back to thank him for speaking up, which reminded Biggie that it was OK for him to speak up by growling to say he doesn't like something.

Later, when Biggie was on the sunning rock, the dog came up again and pestered him. Biggie took some deep breaths and imagined the STOP signal to stop so he could think.

Then he remembered that it was OK to speak up by growling, so he growled instead of swatting at the yapping dog.

When he heard Biggie growl, the dog's owner looked over to see what was happening. Then, he saw the dog kicking some dirt at Biggie, as Biggie growled even louder in a mighty roar.

The neighbor then took the dog into his cottage, and Biggie was able to stretch out on the sunning rock in peace, while enjoying the sun. When he looked over at the neighbor's cottage, he saw the dog in the window, whining and looking sad. Biggie was proud of himself because he had stopped to think of a plan that worked to keep him out of trouble.

Later, when the dog came over again, but patiently waited, Biggie thought of a better plan that helped him become friends with the dog. Because the dog waited, Biggie let him use the sunning rock, while he climbed up on a higher rock to sun himself.

To show how much he appreciated Biggie's kindness, the dog brought Biggie one of his dog biscuits. When they saw Biggie and the dog getting along, Scott's family and the neighbor's family had a cookout for them. They roasted hot dogs and marshmallows, which Biggie and the dog loved.

How Biggie "beat the bully" by speaking up

One summer day when Biggie visited the family at the lake, Sara and Scott ran back from taking a walk. A mean dog had scared them and chased them down the road. Biggie ran down the road to find the dog. He was angry and wanted to throw

the dog into the lake to teach him a

lesson.

On the way, he stopped himself by

imagining the <u>STOP</u> signal and took some

deep breaths, so that he could calm down and think about what he should do.

He thought about throwing the dog into the lake. Then Biggie realized the game warden might come and take him to "bear jail," or what humans called a zoo.

Biggie decided to "speak up" instead. When he found the dog, Biggie growled a long and loud warning, and the dog ran off frightened.

Later, the dog's owner came to the family's cottage, and asked, "Why did your bear friend scare my dog?"

Sara and Scott spoke-up and explained that the dog had scared them and chased them down the road. The man apologized and went back to his cottage. Later, when Biggie and the kids took a walk down the road, they saw the dog chained to a tree and looking sad.

Biggie realized that he had "beat the bully" by speaking-up. If he had "beaten-up" the bully by throwing the dog into the lake, he would have lost out in the long run and gotten himself into trouble. By speaking-up to warn the bully, he won!

Remember the message of this story:

If you see someone being bullied,

speak up to a parent or a teacher to

"Beat the Bully."

Be Big Like Biggie:
Stop & speak up!

Stop to think and speak up,
before you blow up!

Biggie-2

After Biggie the Bear went back to live in the woods, Scott and Sara's parents gave them a wonderful dog that reminded them of Biggie, so they named him "Biggie-2."

They liked to play chase with Biggie-2, and he liked it too. They also had many fun adventures with Biggie-2. He would go on long hikes with the kids and play with them in the water.

The parents knew that Biggie-2 would protect the kids from any wild animals or stray dogs that could bother them. Biggie-2 also knew the way home if the kids ever got lost while hiking.

When Biggie came back to the cottage to visit, he also loved to play chase with Biggie-2, and he appreciated that Biggie-2 took such good care of his young friends.

Prologue:

The story about Biggie-2 was included to remember Shadrack, who was a good dog and the real "Biggie-2."

About the Author:

Dr. Bob Peddicord is a Pediatric Psychologist who has worked to help children and parents for over 30 years. He was co-founder of the Child & Parent Center in Bangor Maine.

Biggie the Bear began as the hero of stories Dr. Bob told his son, and he was later included story lessons developed to teach CARES Success Skills. Dr. Bob presented Biggie the Bear CARES story lessons to all the kindergarten and elementary students in two Maine school districts and to various school classes and groups, thanks to a Character Education Grant from the Maine Department of Education and to several school administrators.

To see other publications and programs by Dr. Bob, please go to Amazon.com and search for Dr. Bob Peddicord.

Thanks to:

Thomas Block for the illustrations
of the imaginary Biggie the Bear
& Gail VanWort for the illustration
of Biggie the Teddy Bear

Dedicated to:

My dad, Steve Peddicord, who lived
his life by the principles embodied
in these stories

&

My wife, Bobbie Fine Peddicord,
who loved children, was a wonderful
mother and devoted to our children.

CPSIA information can be obtained
at www.ICGtesting.com
Printed in the USA
LVHW070536280420
654654LV00008B/1681